SCAR CITY

RAY LEIGH

Cover art by dave@hmdesigners.com

Cover design by BAD PRESS iNK

ISBN: 978-1-9160845-1-3

published by www.badpress.ink

For John

On a clear day you can see forever.

From the northern elevation the city spread out in the basin of the Thames.

Aircraft flying downriver.

The commercial sector, the religious buildings.

Damp and grey.

Another elevation, a ghetto funeral.

A hearse and police on a street corner.

A man walks up a parkland hill. The city below him.

Inside the ghetto home, a black man and his wife, elders, pensioners, suffering and wisdom.

He clear now. Clear.

His wife squeezes his shoulder.

Outside they take out the box, coffin.

C L E A R

Up on the parkland hill the white man breathes.
We see his breath in the cold.
An observation point over the funeral.
Police RT chatter.
The white man breathes.
Breath.
Breath.
   It's clear.

The police observation, the helicopter, the city.
The family on the street, respectful, the business associates of the deceased, subdued
and mean.

Inside prison a cell door opens.
A white man joins his escort.
Outside the prison we see his release.
He turns to the guard
I am going all the way.
Clear.
He breathes.

The crowds outside a fashionable shopping area tube station. A smart young black man.
Young women and young men meeting with a kiss.
John greets Shirlon.
She says
Take me back.
This place ain't for me.

C L E A R

Later on, the ghetto streets.

Listen. Them people have nothing for me.
And nothing for you.
You gotta see that.

A government car. A middle-aged man with the power of the state. He gets in outside a white Nash terrace with brass plate.

The man in the back seat opens his briefcase and hands the driver an envelope with cash

It's all day lunch now.

Outside a man is handcuffed beside his car.

A plain-clothes police officer holds the back of his hair and rams his face into the roof of the car. The traffic moves on.

Walking away from the prison. A tatty second-hand shop. DSS welcome. Sean walks in. Bottle of scotch a day. Shop owner aged 55 comes out. There is a small Belling cooker.

Sean

Show me.

Shop man

It all works.

The man pulls the plug cord up and plugs it in. Sean picks up a bread knife and pockets it.

Shop man

You can have it for twenty.

Sean says

I don't care.

Away from the shop towards the bank. Eyeline for the cash point queue.

5

CLEAR

A ghetto off-licence. Grilles over the booze and a Rottweiler.

Shirlon

> *That one (a bottle of pink lady).*
> *And the blue ones (Rizla).*
> *I got a little something.*

On the street.
Two boy-girls huddle in a doorway.
A pimp doesn't get out of his car.
We hear

> *I will get you.*

And see their quiet fear.

The government car outside the restaurant.
He disembarks.

The fingers on the cash point numbers.
A knife across the eyes.
Resting on the inside of the socket.

Sean

Balance.

The finger.

Sean

All of it.

Finger on withdrawal.

The big estate. Security booth. Lift.
Shirlon's sister's place.

She won't be back 'til late.

The view from the balcony.
The city.

C L E A R

The maître de at the restaurant.
The state power man. With briefcase
All day lunch today.
The booth at the back.

Sean in a pub. With exotic dancers.
Two rowdy women at the bar.
Sean to the barman
I promised I'd sort him out.
Barman
I'll take you up there.

Shirlon's sister's place.
John and Shirlon and Lee and Mark.
Sitting on the floor. Smoking and drinking.
Young people laughing. Lee is performing.
Shirlon says

No guy. I got no respect for any black man who goes with a white bitch.
She I can understand. Yes, she wants what is mine. But he – see him – he is eating
pork, unclean see.

John

Babe, sshh, people, man, people.

Lee says

Sister you just squealing 'cos you don't want man to take his pleasure.
If some white thing say come up and thing-man is going to play.

Mark

Them girls is weird, guy.

Lee

Tell she, tell she.

Mark

Them girls they always got some cultural thing there, man. Some Marley thing or some
black guy picture on the wall.

C L E A R

Lee

Scene, scene.

Mark

Yeah, man. You digging some girl and you got some brother looking down at you.

Lee

Yeah man.

And they want to play some reggae tune.

Mark

And smoke your weed.

Lee

And suck your dick.

[Laughing]

Mark

Yeah man, them girls.

Lee

I gotta tell them it ain't no lollipop.

John is uneasy.

Mark

No disrespect, brother.

Lee

    Naah, man. No disrespect.
    Hey chill, chill.

Another suit bustles through Soho.
Into the restaurant. Another power merchant.
Top men shake hands.
    School house.
    School house.

Sean and the barman out of the pub.
A dosser smacks his female partner in the face.
They cross the road where the junkies wash car windscreens.
They go into some flats.
A fortified door.
A man with a shaved head opens it.

C L E A R

Two youths loiter outside an expensive watch shop.
One breaks away. The other slides down the street.
An Arab businessman leaves the shop.

Laughter and giggles.
John feels uneasy. Too much slack talk.
Shirlon and John.
Shirlon
  Go for another wine.
Passing a note into his hand.
A moment of fear.

The government men demand a different waiter.
Suits power tripping.

Public toilets at a railway station.
Sean leaves his outer garments in a cubicle.
Washes thoroughly in the sink. Arms, torso, face.
A fat wedge of cash.
Flecks of blood all over his face.
An effective clean up.

John dithering by the front door.
Opens it and then goes into the toilet.
Tense. The front door slams shut.

The youths follow the businessman down the shopping street. Through the crowds.
A keen eye on their prey.
Surveillance.

CLEAR

Sean in the cubicle.
Flicks through the cash. Pockets it.
Opens packet of coke.
Tastes it.
Pockets it.
Rummages through garments.
Cleans knife with jacket.
Covers with cloth and tucks in belt.

Breathes.
Breathes.

John out of the toilet.
Checks money. Dithers.
Goes back to the quiet laughter and giggles.
Jungle music.
The city through the high-rise window.
John checks the view.
Movements in the high-rise car park.
The motorway.

CLEAR

Aperitifs. The men in the restaurant.
Cufflinks and crisp shirts
  Jackets off, I think.
Significant, isn't it
  God yes, jackets off.
Jackets off and one smirks
  All I really remember is that gorgeous blond boy.
  And you running around after him.
  I think we all ended up with shit on our dicks.
  Didn't we?
    All day lunch and jackets off.

    More.

The businessman gets off the bus.
One youth is downstairs. One is up.
He walks away past the railings.
One youth bounces into him.
Face to face
  What is it?
Hard faced. The businessman hard too
  Move.

The second youth from behind.
Hand on his arm.
A craft knife to his throat
  Don't be stupid.

The second fumbling with the watch strap.
The businessman makes to struggle.
A smack in the mouth.
The watch off.
They break away. Running.
Then walking. Separate sides of the street.

17

C L E A R

John watching the city. The view from the high-rise. Flashing blue lights. Movement.

Back into the room. No laughter or giggles.

Shirlon's head in Lee's groin.

She disengages.

Looks at John.

Saliva wet on her lips.

Horror.

The horrors.

A crowded gay bar.
Leathers and rings and trade and rent.
Amyl nitrate and pumping, pumping.
Sean at the bar.
Young acolyte at his side.
He passes him a twist of coke.
And says
        I'll come back to yours.

John out on the street.
Wide-eyed.
A police van passes.
All eyes on the black man.
Another street.
Home.
A bed in a tiny room.
A tenor pan.
John plays a riff. Then sits on the bed.

C L E A R

Night.
The homeless boy-girls snug in the doorway.

Sean stands by the window. Dawn over the city.
Unclean. A shower cubicle.
Rent. Trade.

Acolyte
Jesus, don't you ever fucking sleep?

Sean
Not much.

John dresses for work.
Collar and tie. Mirror.
Picks up pan stick. Drops it.
Out into the street.

In the restaurant. A napkin over the mouth.
A little garlic butter from the side of middle-aged lips. A little drunk.
   They'll always be there.
A pause, meaning, Who?
   The great unwashed.
Wine is refilled.
      You can see criminals at nursery school.
   Breeding.
         People can beat their history you know.
   Not many.
         How do you feel about ties?
   Could loosen.
      Loosen.
         Jackets off.
      All day lunch.
   All day lunch.

C L E A R

A West Indian Community Centre.
Steel band practice. [Mangrove, Glissando.]
Young musicians under tutelage.
Let's go.
Into a tune - ragged at first.

1930s tenement block - balcony flats.
A young woman; short skirt, bare legs, knee high boots, bomber jacket with two carrier bags.

The steel band leader.
Stop. Exasperated.
Show them, John.
John plays.

The door to the flat is opened.
A heavy-set woman of forty.
Straight wool dress. Cigarette. Swollen feet in court shoes.

The pan stick on the drum.
The tune.

CLEAR

Inside the flat.
Liam is fifty. A building contractor
    Mary, we go back a long way.
        Aye we do. We do.
Drink. Cigarettes. Ashtrays full. TV on.
Stereo on.
The young girl and another like her sat on the couch.
Mary on her feet
    Come on now, Liam. Come on now.
Liam is getting up.

The steel band.
    One more time.
The tune.

The two girls holding glasses of whiskey.
Liam on his feet with his arm around Mary.
Mary with a cigarette and a vodka.
Liam pathetic in his drink

You're a wonderful woman, Mary.

Aye sure, sure now, Liam. Now.

Mary you know how to live, don't you now?

Aye. Liam. What is it?

Mary, Jesus, I need to rest.

I'm well full.

Aye, Liam. You can lie down on my bed.

Mary, you're a wonderful woman.

Have you fifty pounds now?

Aye, here you are.

Brigid will bring a drink.

Ah, Mary.

Liam, do whatever you want. No rush now, do whatever you want.

Liam goes into the next room. Brigid follows.
The door shuts. Mary sits down. The other girl glances at Mary.
Mary

C L E A R

I don't know what you're looking at neither, you dirty little whore. You've not brought a penny into this house for three fucking days.

The steel band. They stop.
The tutor goes to John
Tell your father you're the best I've ever seen.

Sean and the acolyte in second-hand Jaguar.

On the urban freeway.

The Acolyte - moaning

I want to do something.

Sean looks at him.

Hard.

The car pulls over.

Sean

Fuck off.

Acolyte with questions in his eyes.

Sean

Fuck off.

The car pulls away.

C L E A R

John goes to work.
Swish media company offices.
Settles at desk.
Tries to focus.
Young sales woman puts coffee on his desk
I do look after you, don't I?
in mock intimacy. Saliva on her lips.

Her mouth.

A taxi outside a council children's home.
Mary and the geyser on the back seat.
I'll only be a minute.
Mary out of the cab. Compact out. Wiping off make up with tissues.

John. Throws coffee over desk.
Looks at fearful woman
You is nasty.
Man, you is nasty.
A silence around the room.
John

I come to this place to work.
Then some bitch come push herself in my face.
You is pigs. Nasty, unclean, pigs.
A moment's realisation.
Jacket on. Walking proud.
By the door. Parting
I is man. Yous are nothing.
I is man.
A stunned quiet.

CLEAR

A social worker greeting Mary at the door.
Mary is full of drink but handling it.
The social worker blathers nervously

Oh Mary, we weren't expecting you.
Sean will be pleased to see you.
You haven't been for ages – have you?
He's much more settled now.

Mary   *Aye well let me see him then.*

John back in the family home. Sitting in a chair.
His father standing
What happen? No work?

John

    I can't take these people.
    I can't take them.
       You ain't working.
    I finish.
       You got something else?
    I don't know.
       Go now.

John stands and leaves.

Mother

    That girl she done him something.
    She done something, I know.

A child of nine in front of Mary.

Aye, Sean. Give us a kiss.

She stoops, a little uncertain with the drink.

He kisses her cheek

Did Brigid bring you some fags?

He nods

They got me a camera for me birthday.

Mary

Aye, she told me. Go and get it.

In the cab she hands the camera to the punter.
Sean sits in front of the TV pulling on a fag.
University Challenge is on.

The lunch in the restaurant.
It's actually chaos.
Complete chaos. A zoo with the cages open.
Exert a little pressure. Maintain the perimeters.
Let the dogs eat the bloody dogs.

33

CLEAR

John on the frontline.
Eating a roti. Watching a few moves.
Police surveillance from overlooking flats.
An officer inputs car registrations.
Spilt screen video monitoring the street.
Hopkins enters wearing a woollen hat. Breezy.
With him another officer, younger and black.
Melody

What's happening down on the farm?
The officer inputting

I logged Bootsy all last week.
Definitely a man possessed.
Another officer

Banjo's back. Making little moves.
Not much else.

Come on, let me have a go.
Hopkins operates the video surveillance.
Zooms in on the faces. Rastas and hoods.

Briefly scans John, muttering
Got to mind the young ones.
Hopkins drawing away from the screens
OK, good work.
Listening kit next week.
And interpreter.
Questioning looks
I don't understand monkey.
Deliberately regardless of Melody.
Back to the screens. In control.
Homing in on some dumped rubbish
Send a plod to have a look.

C L E A R

Two white youths outside an expensive house.
Tense, waiting.

It's alright, he's got the bottle.

Two uniform officers move from a street corner
And down the line. We see from the surveillance.
We see Sean, aged nine, opening the door of the house.
The youths go in.

The police have found a body.
A deranged Rasta with a placard around his neck is making a speech

The Babylon done this.
The Babylon and the white's man wickedness has done this. We still in the
plantation.
This is more cane we cutting. Still.
And them government men want this ghetto thing.
And this drug thing and they want us to die in their Babylon.

Hopkins

It must be on the fucking tapes.

I got fucking arseholes sitting up here twenty-four hours a fucking day and then I come and there's a fucking stiff on my fucking street while you fucking pratts are paid to keep the fucking place clean.

I don't want notorious drug dealing area.

I don't want frightened fucking residents.

I want this shit cleaned up.

Clean it up...

A minicab outside the expensive house.

The driver radios control

8-0-7 outside.

37

CLEAR

Deranged Rasta

They want to give us powders and they want to give us rock and they want to destroy our spirit and destroy our culture and they want us to live like animals – the white man and the white man's wickedness is here now, this is Babylon.

He has pieces of lighted paper which he waves as if to ward off spirits.

Hopkins

Now I look like a cunt.
A million-pound operation going on.
I don't know. I don't know.
You're the fucking cunts, aren't you?
What have you been doing up here?
What have you been doing?
Look at me.
You're a pair of cunts.

He turns to Melody

And you're just another fucking nigger.

C L E A R

The phone rings inside the house.
The youth picks it up.
We hear
    Cab's outside, mate.
We see Sean and the youths load holdalls into the car.

The government men in the restaurant
We're doing what we can.
    Keeping the lid on.
    How do you feel about a bit of whoring?

It is dark.

Infra-red observation.

John on the line. Special brew. An older black guy.

Rasta

What happen, bro.

Thinking about some tea.

You have ten pounds?

John shows the note

You Sugar, man?

Sure, I'm Sugar.

In a doorway, bag of sugar. Full of weed.

A betting slip – Sugarman puts a pinch of weed on the slip.

John

I take two sugars.

Sugar

You take nothing, brother. I give you.

Two.

Move your rasclat, boy.

Two.

41

C L E A R

Sugar tells him

See you. You're going to meet my brother, man.
My brother.
    Who that?
    Char. Move.
        Two.
My brother is going to teach you bunderclat respect.

John is unmoved

    Who he then?
    Bring him in.

Sugar

My brother with me always.

John

    You talk shit.

A little attention and tension around the two men.

We hear

    That youth got no respect.
    Let Sugar deal with it.
    He's going to get some serious licks.

Sugar

You still here?

John

I'm going nowhere.

Sugar

Sure?

A machete drops from Sugar's sleeve into his hand.

Next time, boy, you bring something for my brother here.

John is moving away.

We hear

Look, he walk like a white man now.

Sugar, your brother look hungry man.

That youth going to cry, man.

Hey yo – send your woman next time, bro.

I know she, she sweet, send her, send her, man.

43

C L E A R

Sean in gay bar, working class.
Tacky rent boy.
Sean

   Can you drive?

John in park – Meanwhile Gardens.
Scruffy. Head in hands.
Opposite on a bench. Angel.
Exchange of smiles.
From somewhere the tune.

The Jaguar at a telephone box.
The rent boy driving.
Sean goes to the box and takes out all the prostitutes' cards.
He starts calling on his mobile.

C L E A R

Angel

It can't be that bad.

John

It's worse.

Angel

Is someone dead?

John

Me, inside.

Pause.

Angel

You want to get a grip, mate.

John

Is it?

Angel

Yeah. Tidy yourself for a start.

The words are dancing. Something's happened. Just playing roles while the love arrives.

He says

Yeah.

With mockery and unfazed, she says

Yeah. Get a grip. Tidy yourself up.
You're probably a nice guy.
      And you would know, would you?

Well.

            I'll be here tomorrow.

I might pass by.
            Might you?

Yes, I might.
      What is your name?

Angel.
            Yours?

      John.

She says
      John.

He says
      Angel.

Love that aches too much.

Angel
            I'm going.

C L E A R

John

I know.
  Stay with it.

The suits in the restaurant
They actually consume one another.
  Like crowded rats.
I read clinical psychology.
  Exactly the same.

Sean close to the woman's face.

Her

Let's call it eighty, then.
  Ssshh.

A hand on her face.
A razor blade between thumb and finger.

Late night on the frontline.
Police observers yawning
    Party time over.
Scanning the line
    Almost.

The razor nicks some skin.
A little blood.
Sean

    Are you going to be sensible?
    Or can I cut you up?

CLEAR

We see Sugar walking away from the line.
John is half a block behind.

Sean gets in the car and throws some money and a purse in the glove compartment.
He gets out the phone - checking the cards.
He looks at the driver

I'm going to do two more.

John's trainers on the pavement.

Sugar fumbling for keys.

John comes from behind.

He hits him with a sock filled with sand.

Released athletic power.

Sugar

What the...?

John

I have no brothers.

He hits him across the jaw with the cosh.

Sugar goes down.

John goes straight to his pocket and lifts the sugar bag.

C L E A R

We see the moon over the city.

The homeless in the doorways. The Hare Krishna food van and a queue of hungry dirty men.

Night buses and Trafalgar Square.

Boats on the Thames. The second-hand Jaguar in the West End and a young black man walking the ghetto streets.

The restaurant.
Christ look at the time.
    You can't see it.
What?
    Time.
I suppose not.
    It just goes by.
God, and don't we change. Hey.
    Don't we.
Can't have it back you know.
    No, can't get it back.

C L E A R

And ten years pass. Ten more years. Ten years after.
Ten years in the darkest night.
And now in the first light of dawn.
Dawn over the city. The sky lightens.
The sun rises to show us this pain.

John strides across his luxury bedroom.
Through the patio doors a large garden.
He wanders into the kids' bedroom. They sleep unknowing. Half-dressed he goes to bed.
Angel stirs. Love in his eyes.
The love story.

Hopkins in a hotel room. Five star and he's up with a towel around his fat belly. Unsteady into the bathroom. The sound of urination. And back to the sleeping whore on the bed.

Beautiful and half-exposed.

Melody turns over and snuggles up to his wife who holds a child in her arms. They all sleep on.

Through dawn.

C L E A R

Sean in his flat overlooking the park. Another boy in his bed. He runs his finger down the nape of his neck.

He kisses him and then sneers

Aren't I the best thing that has happened to you?

Then crossing the room, he settles in the armchair.
Toying with a gun and zapping the TV remote onto the Open University.

John sits on the bed. Angel stirs and reaches for him.
The large windows letting in grey light. Beside her their faces close. Their lips meet. And just open, and a split second of passion and he pulls away. And he turns away. His hand wipes across his lips. Uncertain.
Angel hurts. And flops back onto her pillow.
Hurting.

Hopkins, a shaking hand on the whore's back.
Searching for something, a response. She doesn't care. Work's finished and now she
covers her flesh.
His hand on her shoulder squeezing. She speaks with no feelings
    Leave me alone, prick.

John driving away from the house. Angel by the door watching. Just dawn.
And then the clear road into the city. The car change at Uncle's house from the family
saloon to a blacked-out Mercedes. And the clear city streets. And the urban green heath
where the boxer is training. John's moves. John's runnings. John's work. A little
business.

57

C L E A R

Sean asleep in the chair. The gun held in his lap.
Quantum physics or algebra from the tube in the corner.
And light outside. Light now.

John on the mobile
I'm just coming up.

The car draws up and the window winds down.
Then a hooded figure passes the cash to the boxer.
The car moves away.
John back on the phone. Working the streets.

Sean twitches in the chair. Quite viciously disturbed and then settles.

But twitching again.

Behind his eyes the therapist saying to the child who's playing with small dolls

Who's that, who's that?

and the child frozen for a moment, shocked to say

Mummy.

in Sean's male voice before we see the child's teeth clamped on the doll's neck and the child's hand rips off the body. Decapitation.

Sean starts. Awake and sweating.

C L E A R

John on the mobile

Where he? Where he now?

Hard and unflinching. The boxer clocking him from the corner of his eye.

A complication. Someone not where they should be.

The Mercedes outside an address.

The boxer

Let me go for it.

John

No, you mind this.

closing the glove compartment.

Melody arriving at work. Into the underground car park with a

Good morning, sir.

and down plush corridors close to the centre of power.
On his way up to a room with a view. Everything is clean.
Melody stays clean.

In the hotel lounge a manager approaches Hopkins

Sir, is there a problem?

Hopkins shows ID deliberately and engages the manager's eyes

There is a prostitute in room 113.

Get her out.

He looks for the waiter and taps his coffee cup.

C L E A R

Sean paces the room. He windmills his arms and walks up and down circling his head around on his neck.

The gun still in his hand. Then opens a drawer full of pills and takes three.

John is in a room.

A white man and a girl are asleep on the bed.

There is a table with crack pipes and a bottle of rum. There is a thin pimp and two girls.

They're very high.

The pimp is giving John money

It's all there, man. It's there.

Guy, I thought I'd missed you man.

I weren't plotting nothing man, you know that.

And a girl is coming up to John. Hot pants and a top.

Fit and gorgeous. Wrecked and pouting. Her hand flutters towards his groin. She slurs

I am pretty. Aren't I?

John is watching her friend. The pimp is feigning disinterest and sleep. Her friend is dancing. The hand is fluttering. The friend is watching. Pretty girl drops her eyes towards John's groin. And back to him

Aren't I pretty?

And her friend is coming over, is coming over and her hand flutters from shoulder to arse and she's dancing a little and pretty girl says

Ever been kissed by two girls?

Have you... ever?

And her eyes drop to his groin and her friend moves closer and down.

And Angel is taking the kids to the school in the Range Rover and the phone rings and we hear his voice

I love you, I love you.

and she is cool and reassuring

I love you too, I love you too.

And one of the girls says

Is that Daddy, Is that Daddy?

all excitement and Angel

OK, usual time, I will, bye.

CLEAR

And when the vehicle stops, she turns and blows kisses and they try to catch their kisses from Daddy.

Hopkins in the car in the London traffic and mothers and children crossing the street. The children of London, black, white, Asian, oriental, going to school. School gates and Hopkins puffing with impatience.

Hopkins says to the driver's neck

All sorts and half-breeds

Evil fuckers.

C L E A R

Melody has a deputy commissioner in his office

I accept there is a certain sensitivity around some of these issues but drug related crime, I mean supply basically, and its relation to certain communities is proven. It is.

And we need movement on this.

Melody

  Results.

    Exactly.

The deputy commissioner moves towards the window.

A little something now, a little something will move you right up there.

    Thank you, sir.

    This week.

John goes into the property company offices, Shadowlands, with the boxer carrying his bag.

Hopkins arrives at a police station and Angel is pulling away from school.

Close up on the government men in the restaurant

No don't forget us. We'll always be here.

And his friend

Yes, I suppose we're timeless, sort of a constant.

God yes, I do think we are bloody England.

We are bloody England.

CLEAR

The Rolex boys are in a Ford Granada at 70mph.
Up a steep hill. They are screaming. A police car is in pursuit.

Hopkins's governor. Gerry Manley. Sixty and dapper.
Effective. Not clean but presentable.
All's fair in love and war

Only your best friends are going to tell you.

Hopkins

What?

> It's over. You're finished.
> They're saying you're out of control.

Who?

> Upstairs want you gone. Soon.

I'm going to deliver on this.

> Stop that. The squads dissolved. It's all over.

I'll have my man.

Manley shows some intolerance

> Come on get a grip.
> I'll have him by the end of the week.

You're going to have to face it sooner or later. It's that or they'll be escorting you out.

69

C L E A R

In a locked ward. The Rasta man

This government take my woman.
Yeah, they take my woman fill her full of champagne and sell her to some Arab boys.
Scene, scene. Up there in them country house health club, he sell her to them.
Government man, he a pimp.
I know him. I know him.
And he a pimp.

Angel is on her knees scrubbing the fridge.
Its manic and lonely and sad and outside the breeze is in the trees and the suburbs are safe.

Sean is dribbling as he sleeps at the foot of the bed. He turns over and sucks his thumb.

71

C L E A R

Hopkins arrives at Shadowlands.
John is watching from the upstairs window.
Hopkins goes in, unspeaking past reception.
The boxer turns off the TV when Hopkins enters.
John and Hopkins stay standing.

Hopkins

Where is it?

There. Twenty.

Hopkins, giving orders

By Friday. On Friday pm, I want a nick.
Fair and square. I want a face in possession.
On my patch. Friday.

John

Things ain't that easy.

I'll have the squad. Friday pm.

Get me the face.

Easy, relax.
  You see I need this one.
  Is it? Is it?
    Yes, my friend. Yes.
Hopkins and the package are gone.

Melody in uniform. On the frontline.
A voice from the tension
  Hey, Melody – what tune you play now, man?
  I knows you. Melody what happen?
  Uh huh – Melody like you like them fancy clothes.
Melody's brother officer speaks
  Well known here, sir.
  Small island people, they know everyone.
We hear
  Safe.
  Man, Melody safe, man.

C L E A R

Raider Jim's, a Mayfair bar.
Hopkins entering from the street.
Opulent and corrupt.
Barman and businessman and well, all the rest.
Hopkins arrogant and massive.
Beside him at the bar Sean.
Sean unmoving.
Hopkins clocks him

I know you.

    Do you?

Hopkins drinking and thinking. And looking around and then at Sean. A smile comes on his lips

I know exactly.

Sean unfazed

    Oh yeah?

Hopkins looks around. The bar is his. His kingdom

You were the little toe rag that turned over some of Julie's girls.

    You sure?

Hopkins drinks. It has a tiny effect

I don't forget.

Really.

Sean feels safe.

No, I don't forget.

Hopkins drinks. Indifferent to him.

Angel wiping shelves.

Melody outside the Caribbean restaurant.

The owner outside. A little charade.

Melody

Good morning.

From the restaurant

Man, cool.

Can I come inside?

And the man steps aside.

Hopkins struggling
I don't forget.

Sean

Of course you don't.

Hopkins

I know what happened.
It was sorted. I know…

Inside the restaurant a brief snatch of
They call him the Shadow.
He's the number one guy. The shadow.
East. I think he's East.
and then Melody
I'm pleased things are going well for you.
Always remember these are licensed premises.
Somehow not making sense. But a function.

Hopkins

It was sorted. We had a word and Julie let it go. You did something for her and that was it.

Sean looks up at him

No.

   I had a word with Julie.
   And you got off my back.

Hopkins looks at him. Sean remains steady.

Sean

   I know she owns you.

The government men. Close up still. Lips some food debris.

   There is so much trash around now.

C L E A R

The winos drinking, the homeless in doorways, the poor at the bus stop, the lo-cost supermarket, the high-rise estate, the communal play areas, the security systems, the queue outside the post office, the cheap shoe shop and the line of hungry men waiting for soup. Faces in the market and the young in the West End. Buses and tubes London, England and written on the road *Keep Clear*.

Shadowlands.

John

I'm away.

The boxer

That man.

John

He the captain of the slave ship.
He the son of the son of one of them.
He part of this glorious land.
That man is England too.
Isn't he?

The air is heavy. Anger released.
I'm going to Angel.
Vulnerable. A little shaken. Almost less strong.

C L E A R

Melody at his desk. His laptop computer open.
A phone at his ear. The keyboard and faces appear.
Three black men on the screen.

    Rogers, Melody.

        Sir.

The finger on return.

    I've sent you three faces this afternoon.
    I want them in the nick by four.
    They are all on the Mozart.
    It's a red operation.

        Sir.

    Two pm go.
        No problem.

Hopkins tapping his glass. Sean in conversation with someone else. Faces in the lounge. The smell of money.

The blacked-out Mercedes. Shadow in the outskirts.

The car change at Uncle's house. We hear Uncle.

He says as he takes the keys

You finish early.

The force preparing.

Melody faces the attack plan.

Targets.

The dressing up. The camaraderie.

The squad. The smell of action.

Armour. Bullets. Weapons. Telecommunications.

Vehicles.

The chopper is fired up.

C L E A R

Hopkins drinks. Sean finishes his conversation and turns back to the bar
You still here?
I wasn't planning on leaving. [Almost girlish.]
Hopkins a little unsure.
I don't think I like you.
Sean almost smiles.

Angel on her knees sweeping dust and dirt into a dust pan.
John is approaching the house.
Angel stands up.
The key in the door.
John comes in.
Angel straightens herself.
John puts a box with a gold ribbon on the table.

The helicopter is in the air.
The personnel carriers position around the estate.
CID drift in. Melody puts on Mozart.
Tape hisses.

Hopkins drinks. It has a tiny effect.
He looks around. Sean smiles. He looks away.
Sean says
Maybe you're beginning to like me now.

John reaches into the box.
Angel says
Let me get a plate.
Angel goes to the cupboard.
John puts back the cake and stands behind her.
He kisses her neck. So, and a bit more.
It reaches her.
She takes the plates to the table.

Mozart.

Melody's laptop. Mozart.

Feet on gas pedals. Exhaust pipes. Grinning coppers.

Happy plods getting some action. Here we go.

Feet on walkways running.

Doors going down, guns and shields. And over there another one going down.

Into the houses.

In.

Police yell

Mind the kids.

In the house.

Hopkins drinks. Damaged by it now

Is it me you want?

Hopkins looking up

Who are you?

Sean pushing himself forward. And smiling.

Hopkins trying to recover.

CLEAR

John behind her. He nibbles her neck.
A little forward over the table.

Close up rough stuff inside the house.
The helmet. The shield.
The screaming, the manacled men on the floor.
Always half-dressed and fleshed.
The sense of accomplishment.
Man hunt complete.

Sean
I'm the end.
The end.
Hopkins all ears.

Angel is sitting down eating her cake.
John paces. He looks. She's got cream on her lips.

Melody in the cells.
He goes up to the spy hole. Taps it with his pen
I will take note of any co-operation I receive.
I want Shadow.

For a moment Hopkins looks in Sean's eyes.
Sean laughs back.
Maybe I could help you.

John takes off his jacket. Walks into the lounge.
Reclines on leather sofa. Relaxes. Angel at the table
Angel come here.

C L E A R

Melody at the spy hole.
Taps his pen. We see the man.
Taps his pen. We see another man.
Taps his pen. Lips against the spy hole
They say he went to St Augustine's.
Melody's lips
You won't go down.

Hopkins
  You like money.
Sean
  Sesame street.
Hopkins
  But I'm not sure what you do.
  I wonder what a little toe rag like you does.
  Especially if you need to come in here.
  Bottoms up - as they say.
  I can smell a pimp. You know, smell one.
Sean
  Bamber Gascoigne.
Hopkins drinks.

C L E A R

Melody at St Augustine's school. The headmaster on the front steps. Melody confident.

Commander Melody

Commander Melody. [Introducing himself.]
Headmaster we're running a very important operation.
Quite crucial.

They are inside. A long school corridor.
Children's poetry on the walls.

Headmaster

Poetry.
My pet passion.

Melody scans one or two

Voices in the wilderness.

Headmaster

But for them to have a voice.
It's so much.
Don't you think?

John

 Angel come here.

 Come.

Angel

 Why?

John

 Because I love you.

There is a breeze across the garden.
Magpie on the lawn. Quiet suburban sounds and a sense peace. A car, a lawnmower,
and a jet plane high above. She goes to him and kneels beside him.

91

C L E A R

Angel
I know that you're close to the end.
He twists his head away. Shame fills him.
Tears in his eyes. He shifts on the couch.
Angel
We'll be alright We'll make it.
John turns to face the back of the couch.
He knows she sees his weakness. She sees his failure. He lets out an audible breath slowly.
Closing his eyes and then back to her, suddenly intense and fearful
You're clear. And the kids. You're clear.

In the headmaster's office.

Melody

We need to go back fifteen or twenty years.

The headmaster is paying attention.

I have a year photograph – every year.

The old school teacher is looking round the walls at the faces from the past. Lines of youth getting the school photo done, year after year. Melody is working

I'm looking for a certain sort of child, Headmaster. I'm looking for the best Black students in each year.

Headmaster

There's so much talent.

So much.

93

C L E A R

In the bar there is a group of businessmen, four of them.
With a professionally dressed woman.
Jacket and slacks.

With her another woman. Skirt and high heels.

Flirtatious and pouting.

Hopkins is watching. So is Sean.

The professional woman introduces her friend.

Hopkins drinks.

The oldest game.

   New tricks, old dogs.

   You don't know.

   What it's like to love a whore, smiles Sean.

Hopkins drinks.

Angel kisses John's neck. His hand plays with her hair.
She strokes his cheek.
Let me cook something.

Headmaster. Tired by the memories.
I don't know what happened to him.
Pen on photo.
He won the poetry prize.
He was the very best.

CLEAR

Hopkins

    You see I lost my heart to them.

Sean

    Really.
    Did you?
    You've got nothing left have you?
    The magic roundabout.
    You're on pills.
    I think I'm damned.

Angel is washing rice.
John behind her again. Hands on hips.

Love.

It should be enough.

Shouldn't it?

Angel half sighs. Shifts a little against him.
John

Don't you think.

It's enough, isn't it.

Angel?

Angel rests her back on him

Something's going to break.

C L E A R

The river through the city. Almost a sewer between high sides and tides and
currents around bridges.
Little beaches and disco boats, sights for tourists, the kids in the parks,
the playgrounds and the streets.
Red buses, black taxis, dirty air and grime, London.

Hopkins unsteady on his feet on the bridge looking out.
On the phone calling. The calm reassurance of her voice.
Hopkins quavering. Quavering
I need some company.

The headmaster triumphant

I keep copies. The ones I like. My favourites.
The very best. Their age gives them something.
Purity. A vision. Here.

John reads the poem, we hear the beats.

THE POEM

C L E A R

The gay club. The music. The boys in shorts.
The leather guys. The sleazy guys. The young guys.
The old men. The ill. The drugged, the drunk and the smiles and the greeting.
Sean in his place.

Simon

You're mean and moody, are you.

Sean

You're too pretty and too nice.

Simon

Treat me right and I'll take you home to tea.
Promise.
I'd go anywhere with you, I would.
You're very brave.
Well love is – isn't it?
How would I know?
Come on. Let me in.
Tea?

Yes, I'll take you.
When?
Tomorrow.
You can meet my mum.

CLEAR

John at the table
Nothing's going to break.
Angel turning around
There's another way.

John

Is there?

Angel

You can turn it around.

Can I?

What?

Stop it.

Stop it?

What have I done?

You don't know?

No.

I thought you had the answer to everything.

It's easy. You're clear. The kids are clear. One hundred per cent clear. OK. Guaranteed.

Us?

C L E A R

On the bridge.

Hopkins

Who is she?

Can I call her?

The evangelist appears. He's American

You can call Jesus

Anytime, twenty-four hours.

Hopkins, disturbed

Fuck off.

Jesus offers redemption and forgiveness – to all the world's sinners

and for all the world's sins.

Are you involved with the devil?

Don't.

You can call at my church. I have the number.

Don't come near me.

And Hopkins holds his head up against the night.

Melody at home. At the kitchen table.
Sharon fussing

So Melody is a happy man tonight?

I had a good day. It ran sweet all the way through.

And?

The only way is up.

Vice in London. The call boxes. The model signs, the escort girls, the street girls, voices on the phone

He's OK. He's always drunk.

But give him nothing in the morning.

I'm serious – whatever he says – nothing.

Call me at one.

C L E A R

The clubs and the bars, the lost and the lonely.
Smiling faces of the young innocent.
And the lost everywhere.

Post-coital, Sean and Simon. His arm over his shoulder. Sean looks childlike.

Simon

I've never seen you like this.

Sean

No.

Simon

No. [Kisses his head.]
What are you thinking about?

Sean

Tea tomorrow.

Melody at his desk – at home, in a dressing gown.
Late. Sharon at the door. Melody with his laptop.
Things so good you can't sleep?"
Go ahead. I'll be there.
That quiet intimacy of a couple preparing to sleep.

Angel
I'll cut your fucking heart out before you leave me.
Angel has a knife.

Hopkins fumbling with the phone.
Hiya. This is Sally.
Who am I speaking to?
He smiles and a peace descends on him.

C L E A R

Angel

No, it's not going to be alright.

You want it easy.

You want to walk away from this.

John

I don't want to go anywhere.

I don't want to go anywhere.

Now, but...

Look I'm not in control.

So everything's fucked.

No.

And I'll be alright?

Yes.

Angel throws a bottle of red wine against the wall

So it's fuck you time, is it?

We can make it.

But no guarantees for you.

I'm OK, the kids are OK, but Daddy...

Daddy's fucked it all up.

John grabs her arm and bangs it against the table. The knife falls. Breaths
and close faces.

Angel

> There is no we.
> There is no us.
> You can't be Daddy if you don't make it.

Some tears and he releases her a little.

> John, don't let this happen.
> Don't.
> Everything will end.

A kiss on her forehead.

John

> I'll make it.
> I'll be there.

Her head on his shoulder.

> It's all dust.

A sob and, sshh.

109

C L E A R

Hopkins on the phone from the hotel room
Champagne.
Smiling, and Sally in her underwear and high heels.
Sally, Sally.
Whaaaat.
You are gorgeous, really gorgeous.
She drinks and consumes the compliment.

The second-hand Jaguar on the quiet suburban streets.
Simon
Here. This is it.
Time for tea.

Hopkins
    And two glasses.
Smiling, and Sally in her underwear and high heels.
    Sally, Sally.
        Whaaaat.
    You are gorgeous, really gorgeous.

C L E A R

Melody at his laptop. Typing. A heading.
'Dis-establishing Crime as a Life Choice'
A wry smile. The ESCAPE button.
Melody presses Escape. The screen dissolves.
Escape.
Screen dissolve.
Escape.
Dissolve.
He picks up the poem.
We hear the beats.

John's hand wrapped in Angel's hair.
Hot faces. Her head still against a little pain.
Tell me you want me.
Tell me.
    John.

Outside the house. Sean and Simon leaving.
Simon's mum.

Sean, give me a kiss.

He stoops.

You're a lovely young man. Look after my Simon.

He kisses her cheek.

She says, handing him a Tupperware box.

There's some cake for you to take home.

Bring back the box – next time you come.

Sally circles Hopkins in underwear and high heels.
Drinking champagne and taunting a little –

What do you want then? What do you want?

C L E A R

The heading.

'Drug Related Crime in UK Ethnic Minority Communities'

Escape.

Escape.

'An Analysis of Conviction Rates for Drug Supply by Racial Group'

Escape.

Escape.

'Crime and Race: A Review of Statistical Methodology'

Escape.

Escape.

Melody in front of the mirror. A comb through his hair.
His hand across his chest. He picks up a small drum.
And sits drumming quietly by the window.

Angel
  I want you.
  John, I want you.
As they make love.

C L E A R

Simon chattering excitedly. The Jaguar on the motorway.

> She really liked you, Sean.
> And it was so nice. Going together.
> You and me visiting family.
> Wasn't it?

The car stops.

Sean

> Fuck off.

Simon almost tearful

> Sean, don't. What is with you?"

Sean

> Fuck off, pratt.
> Why?
> Because I'm the end.
> Alright.
> I'm the end.

The car pulls away. The cake box bounces down the carriageway.

Sally. Wheedling in Hopkins' face

Come on. Tell me.

What would you like?

I'm a big girl. I'll do what you want.

Hopkins pulling himself together.

Holding himself awash on a sea of booze.

Struggling.

I want to sleep, Sally.

Just sleep with my arms around you.

Sally, let me.

C L E A R

Sweaty hair on Angel in the crook of John's arm.

Can't you tell me.

Tell me what it is.

Talk to me.

John?

   I haven't the words.

Coward.

   No. Angel, I've seen too much now.

   Too much to tell.

Pulling away. From a distance we see them sitting in the half light on her bed. Side by side.

John's head down. Her arm around him. His speech uncertain. A little incoherent. Gaining strength.

   It's a spiritual thing.

   It's what happens when there is no hope.

   The way people are – what they'll do.

   It's not just poverty. It's more what's inside.

   So much darkness. Forever finding new lows.

   And what I do. What I do.

It's an affliction. Seeing it means bearing it.
All this I've built is as rotten as me.
I can't bear it any more.
They'll do anything. For so little. For nothing.
It's got so my flesh is infected with it.
I don't want to bring it home.
I don't want to smear it all over you.
It's got between us. I can't get clean, Angel.
I can't get clean. Never. I'll never get clean.
Poverty and poverty of the spirit.
That's what's happened. I'm sorry.

   Tomorrow.
Tomorrow?
   Tomorrow, come to school.
   Come and see the girls at school.
I will.

CLEAR

Melody drumming at dawn.

The second-hand Jaguar on an urban freeway.
A cyclist ahead. Working out through the city dawn.
Impact and the body in the air. Sean, a slight smile.
Mumbling

The end, the end.

Hopkins, his arm reaches out.
She's gone. An old man in an empty room.
Walking naked. Disorientated. Betrayed.
On the mirror. 'Party, girls' party.' In lipstick.

John heavy with grief.
Angel
    You'll come back.
John
    I'll be back.

And on the streets women let you inhabit their flesh for a bag of heroin.
Children sleep in doorways.
The demented and the deranged on every corner and a grey day emerges.

C L E A R

At Uncle's house the car change. And Uncle is there.

The bull been tearing up the line chasing Shadow.

   How so?

See, this Melody.

This man bust down the line and then he bust up the Mozart. This Melody say he want the Shadow.

   Melody?

Melody a brother, man.

He bull, he Babylon, he police.

And he want the Shadow.

   Uncle.

   Uncle what?

    This going to end soon.

   I know that.

Sharon opens the door on the quiet drumming
What's this?
  I can't find no sleep tonight.
  I can't. I'll go in early.
You OK?
    Sure, things coming clear now.

We see the children's handclapping.
We see Hopkins pacing the empty room.
Porn on the TV.

The Rasta in hospital
  Procurement. Procurement.
  Minister for procurement.
    I know him.

123

Melody dressed in the uniform of Senior Police Officer. Drumming.

The boxer on the hill. His breath.

The Mercedes through a tunnel, swerving.

Sean pulling a driver out of a car and beating him.

The children's handclaps.

John to the boxer
The final round.
    Yeah.
    Yeah, I finish.
        Yeah, the end.

Hopkins shaving. Electric. Attention to detail.
Extreme close up. Unmoving.
Extreme close-up. Unmoving.

Sean eating egg, chips and beans in a breakfast cafe.
Ketchup on the egg. Dip the chips. Red on yellow.
Chewing. Masticating the egg and the chips and the beans.

Melody at the front door. Holding the laptop.
Tucking the bongos under his arm. His cap in the other.

Hands passing money. And the government man.
His lips. His voice
What's in it for me?

The Mercedes at Wellington Arch.
John gives the boxer some money
Clear?
  I clear.

Melody through Hyde Park Corner.
The police driver unmoved by the drumming from the back.

Hopkins clipping his nose hairs. Then his ear hairs.

Sean in the municipal baths. A backflip into the water.
Playing like a child.

The Mercedes at Shadowlands.

127

C L E A R

Melody drumming down the corridors of power.

Hopkins washing his hands.

Sean in the showers.

John's fingers on the phone.
Melody in the office.
The phone ringing.
The black hand on the receiver.
The black hand on the receiver.
Voices.
Melody.
John.
Handclaps from the children.

C L E A R

Sean picking up in the shower. Soaping himself.
The other guy watching. Shampoo.

Hopkins in an empty office. No calls. No work.
No one. Nothing. A man at a desk.
Hopkins alone.

Sean naked. The young man naked.
Their bodies together. In the toilet.
At the municipal baths.

Hopkins with phone
            I...
Stumbling, unsure. Unable to speak.

A final urgent thrust from Sean.

Melody saying
The protection plan is comprehensive.

John hangs up. Alone in the office.
He opens the safe. It's full of cash.
Then sits behind a desk with his head in his hands.

Hopkins stumbling
I...
I require the squad for an operation tomorrow.

131

C L E A R

Sean

Would you like something to remember me by?
Would you?

Melody drumming in high office.

The phone by Hopkins' ear.
You are no longer authorised.
You know that.
The phone slammed down.

Sean anoints his new lover with a stripe – from ear to mouth
You won't forget me now.

In a wealthy suburb. A Rolex boy kicking an Asian businessman.
Giving it loads.
Blows to the ribs
Fucking Paki.
His colleague struggling to get the watch off.

Melody drumming.

Sean humming. Puts on a tape in the Jaguar.
Candle in the Wind.

Hopkins arrives at Shadowlands.
John sees him from upstairs.
In through reception.

CLEAR

In the suburb. An unconscious body on the driveway.
The guys looking at the watch. Then the car keys in the man's hands. And the
BMW convertible.
Here we go. Here we go.

The children's handclaps.

Hopkins in the office with John.

One on one. Across the table unspeaking.

John gets up, throws the money on the table in front of Hopkins. Hopkins puts his hand on the money – and speaks

I have the feeling our little relationship is drawing to a close.

John regards him.

It's true.

Hopkins considers

At your age with your responsibilities – perhaps twenty years of jail –

should break you.

Don't you think?

I is above you.

Always.

No, I don't think so.

Hopkins puts the money away.

Something's gone wrong with you.

You're forgetting who's who.

I want you to remember.

I am the law.

135

C L E A R

John is steady
Everything has changed.

Hopkins
If I lock you up, you'll come out an old man.
Now be sensible.
You've a family to think of.
I don't want you to go against me.

John, with a neutral

No.

Hopkins
There's a lack of respect here now.
Isn't there a lack of respect?
Very disturbing. Very fucking disturbing.
If you were thinking, John.
I see you were.
Oh, you little toe rag.
You leaving?

You're finished.
Is it?
Yes, geyser.
It's the end.
The end for you.

The handclaps.

The BMW up a steep hill. Fast.

A voice
Hand relief fifteen pounds.

137

C L E A R

A man unconscious on the pavement.

The government man
Power, such an easy thing to grasp.
His colleague
It's always been ours.

Melody on the park bench. Outside Kensington Palace.
John walking up. Melody in shirt sleeves.
John sits down beside him.

Melody

    So.

John

    I'm coming in.

The park in the sunshine. Courting couples. Children.
Children playing. Mothers and fathers.
And children.

Melody

    We'll take care of you.

    Tomorrow.

John

    Hopkins?

Melody

    He yours?

    I just finished with him.

    He's got no back up.

139

CLEAR

He can't do you nothing.
They finish with him too.
    My soul tired now.
I know.
It's over.
I'm going to take care of you now. Offering a hand
John standing up. Looking around.
    One-love.
        One-love.

Sean at Raider Jim's. Hopkins at Raider Jim's.
At the bar. Sean sniffing. Having nose problems.
Hopkins to a woman at his side
  Darling one word from me and you'll never get in here again.
  Please have a drink.
Hopkins turns to the bar and Sean
  On your own, aren't you?
    Always.
  Drink?
    I'll get my own.

Angel is cleaning the cooker.
The radio is on.
Rubber gloves and scouring pads.
A little too intense.

C L E A R

The BMW is smashed against a parked car.
The windscreen is crazed. Stillness.

The paper cup of pills beside the hospital bed.
The Rasta man twisting slowly - semi conscious
I know their names... the corrupt politician.
He call... they call him...

And he rests into sleep.

The windscreen shatters and two youths tear out of it and off the bonnet onto
the street.
A dog unit arrives and armed response.

Sean is dabbing his nose. There is blood on the handkerchief.
Hopkins spots it

You're deteriorating quickly.

Sean inspects the handkerchief

Something you want me to do, is there?

Hopkins drinks.

Low rise flat roof council blocks.
An Alsation dog on the stairs. Along the balcony.
From outside we see the youths jump from block to block.

Free.

143

C L E A R

Sean is talking to Hopkins. With iron in his voice

You see it's not like a drug.

Afterwards you hardly feel any drugs.

Whatever you take.

You can see through everything. Everyone.

You can do whatever you want. It's maximum power.

I can fuck like a bunny for days.

I can pull whoever I want.

Do anything.

People just get out of your way.

You're king. Fucking king.

Hopkins

The money?

Sean

It's not the money.

Thank you.

I want you to know that.

Of course not.

It's all my way clear.

It gives me that vision, see.
Sets me free, makes me something.
It's everything. I love it. I love it.
   Tomorrow.
Tomorrow. You know what they say.
Tomorrow belongs to me.

The government men
I've nearly had enough.
   Me too.
Let's get the whores in.
   Let's get on with it.

C L E A R

John leaves Shadowlands. The Mercedes hits the traffic.
We see all the drivers' faces, the motorbikes and the trucks.
The government men whisk by, drunk in the back seat.
Above a helicopter, a spotter plane, a jet, and the sky.

The Mercedes at Uncle's. Uncle cool
   Yous early. Again.
John
   Old man, I nearly done now.
      Well, how fast you've moved must have made any man tired.
   Tomorrow the last day.
      Sure.
   Tomorrow the end.

Sean in close. Bright eyed. Excited

It's controlling the end.

The end.

It's so fucking sexy.

Maybe you want a go?

Hopkins has a girl on his arm. His hand is playing with her buttock

You're not in control of fuck all.

This is my game. Don't forget.

My game.

Sean

I've told you I love what I do.

So you know I love doing it.

And I'll do it to you or anyone.

Anytime.

    I…

I am out of control you know.

But I will do this for you.

Because I want to.

I want to.

C L E A R

I want to do it.
I'll have the money on the bridge.
Of course you will.

Outside the sauna massage the government car and the government men. The sauna called 'High Society'.
They're drunk. Two drunk men. One to the other
Come on.

The children's handclaps.

John and Angel embrace. Holding tight.

Sean puts his arm around Hopkins

It gets so I could even fuck an old bear like you.

For a moment Hopkins grins.

The Range Rover pulling up outside the suburban school. The young mothers at the gates. Angel, her arm through his, taking him into the building.

CLEAR

Melody at home drumming.
Sharon

    What's this?
        I'm waiting.
    Did you take that to work?
        I did.
    You trying to throw everything away?
        No, I'm waiting.
    For what?
        I'm waiting...

A government man has his arm around the Madam.
Familiar. Intimate. Almost Family
This is my best friend ever.
We've got to look after him.

Melody
I'm waiting to be given the evidence...

The government man. Introductions over. In the Madam's ear
And I want my special. No cry-babies.

C L E A R

Melody

The evidence to convict senior corrupt police officers.

Sharon

But you home playing the rasclat drums.

Melody

Well if my man don't come in....

I guess if... my man don't come in.

He drums.

Angel and the girls in the classroom with John.
He's vastly uneasy. Angel guiding him.
Showing him the pictures on the wall.
And then leaving all together.

A sunset over the city. The river at night.
The underground train and the office workers.
Brick Lane and the light in the window, Princelet Street.
A man, pen on paper. A film camera by the door.

By the patio doors. The sky behind.
John with Angel
I have this appointment.
Everything has changed.
After this I'm clear.

C L E A R

Melody with Sharon

The frightening thing...
The fear is that it goes all the way.
It might be too much to see.
If they is rotten all the way up.
To the top.
If everything is corrupt.
They going to fall on top of me.
See.
If I cut out too much it going to fall.
On me.

The drum.

Glasses clink. Sean and Hopkins.

Tomorrow.

The bridge.

Angel

   You've changed already.
   I can feel you.
   Again.

John

   After tomorrow we're going to be apart.

Angel

   You're back John.
   You're back.
   I'll just wait.
   You're back John.

CLEAR

Sharon

So you playing big man.
Taking risks with our future.

Melody

I'm not playing anything.
This game out of control.
Man here is on his knees.
We ain't playing at nothing.
It with the Gods.

He drums.

Hopkins is drunk. Talking to a bored whore

Of course she never wanted me.
She never really wanted me. Fair enough.
Fair enough. She didn't want me.
I think she never did want me.
It's just she needed me. You see.
For the kids. To get the kids.

John and Angel in one another's arms. On the bed.

Angel

To feel this again. This oneness.

John

This is right.

Sharon

   And what good that drum doing?

Melody

   The darkness.

   Keeping away the darkness.

Sean

   Being how I am...

He puts his arm around Hopkins' neck, gently

   ...means no kiddiewinks. Doesn't it?

   Means I leave nothing behind.

   Nothing.

   After me.

   Zilch.

Hopkins

   I love my kids

Sean

   The end of the line, me.

Hopkins urgently to the whore
  I love my kids.
She turns to him. Proffering her glass.
  Oh, OK, I'll have another then.
He draws back. Lost. Sean laughs
  Fuck knows who my daddy was.
  Probably some scum punter like you.
  I think I'd rather not know.
  Or perhaps.
He looks at Hopkins. Then smiles, satisfied and says
  Daddy.

The government man to the Madam
Who's it going to be?
There are three girls with the men.
Let's get on with it.

Angel and John sleep.

Melody rolls a joint.

Hopkins drunk
I love my kids. I love my kids.
Sean
I bet they don't think much of you.

C L E A R

And dawn again. Where the sun comes up on the last day.
The last day dawns over the city. Movement increases.

━━━◗

Sean is in his flat. A young man paces the room.
Cocaine all over the table. And money.
Sean is high. The guy is high
   That's it, keep walking.
Sean puts on his coat and paces behind the guy.
Approaches him suddenly and pulls out a pistol.
Holds it to his temple.
Repeats. Practicing. Speeding up his approach.
The fast movement. The gun at the temple.

━━━◗

Hopkins getting on top of a whore.
Drunk. Tired. Clumsy. Incompetent.
Grunting. Leaning forward. As if.
As if to kiss a whore –
Who turns away her face –
He thrusts in – saying
   I love my kids you know.
   I love my kids.

Handclaps from the children.

C L E A R

John rising, disentangling himself from Angel's arms.
She stirs.

John

   It's tomorrow now.

Angel

      For who?

John

   For the children.

Handclaps.

Sean. Repeating the gun to the temple.
Laughing

      The end.

Melody rising from his knees.
Putting on his crisp white shirt.
His eyes red.
Sharon in the doorway watching
Prayers now, is it.
Computer finish.
Man pray now.

Hopkins asleep.
The whore removes his arm with distaste.
Gets up and lights up. Mimics
I love my kids, I love my kids.
Picking up the cash from the table.

C L E A R

Handclaps.

John at Uncle's house. The car swap.
Uncle muttering
So you finish.
Everything change now.
Even the youth change now.
The flame gone.
No more petrol bomb.
No hope now. It's all despair.

John
Old man, I free now.
I free.
Clear.

Melody adjusts his tie.
In uniform. Sharon behind him
I play this one with all my heart.
With all my heart.

Sean

The temple. This is your temple.
As in church or God or things.
The temple.
No protection for the brain. Through here.

C L E A R

Hopkins waking. The whore half-dressed
You ain't going nowhere.
OK then. What do you want?
Hopkins quiet. A taunt in her voice
OK what shall I do?
What do you want?
   Get a drink. Sit down.
   I'm paying for your time.
   Sure you are. And my body.
   Anything you want in fact.
   You're paying. Whaaaat?
    Fuck off.
     Go.

The Mercedes on the street.

Sean asleep in the chair.

Melody crisp in his uniform by the mirror.

Hopkins naked and alone stumbling into the bathroom.

Mothers with buggies and children going to school.
Holding hands and playing.
The handclaps in the playground.

169

C L E A R

Melody at the big offices. The underground car park.
The attendant
  Your authorisation is cancelled.
  You cannot bring that vehicle in here.

The Mercedes in the traffic. A police car pulls in behind. John checks it in his mirror.
A police van pulls out, from a side road.
He's blocked.

Sean paces.

Hopkins is alone.

The government man to his colleague
POWER.
And to the Madam
You know what I want,
Get it.

Melody at reception with a senior officer.
Handing him a letter
That's your copy.
You are suspended with immediate effect.

171

C L E A R

The police all over the Mercedes.
John with arms folded. A police hand removing
hand cuffs from their holster. Officers
checking escape routes.

Sean oiling his gun lovingly.

Hopkins shaving in the mirror.

The government man in the arm chair.
The Madam on the phone half-hushed.
None of them will do it.
   Get anyone. Off the street. Anyone.
   Junkies. Anything. You know what it is worth.
   And a cleaner. I 'll need a fucking cleaner.

Melody walking away.
With his drum.

The cuffs. The white hands reaching for John's folded arms. The hands closing.
The twist and the turn and the sudden rotation and he is away down the street running.

CLEAR

Sean's breath as he moves in the chair.
And he rises, saying
Today's the day.

Hopkins trims his nose hairs. And his ear hairs.
He puts powder on his feet before pulling on his socks.

Two rough girls downstairs at the sauna.
Another girl sorting them out something to wear.
A large glass of whisky in each hand.
Madam

I've got some lovely gear if you want a chase.

Hopkins in the empty office. Alone. Unmoving.

Sean leaving the flat. His big coat on.

John sprinting up the stairs to the overhead railway.

The Mercedes being lifted onto a removal truck.
A major operation unfolding.

The train, John on the train.
Above and across the city.

175

C L E A R

Melody on the street. Holding the drums.
Disregarded by passers-by. A street musician nearby.
Holding the drums. A black man on the street –
Holding the drums.
A black man on the street.

The Madam laying out heroin on tin foil
Lovely gear.
He's alright but he likes to get a bit rough.
No screaming or shouting.
I won't pay you if I have to come in.
Here.

She hands them foil and lighter
So no screaming or carrying on.
He doesn't do much. It's over pretty quick.

The girls are inhaling, going unconscious, almost.
The Madam watches. The other girls show fear.

C L E A R

Melody through the crowds. Looking mad.
A mad black man on the street.
Past Harrods.

The Rolex boys at home. A half-furnished council flat.
A woman at the door. Greetings.
She comes in and sits down
I was thinking of getting some rocks.

Hopkins on the phone
My desk is clear.

Sean on the street. A poor area. The poverty.
Under his breath
There ain't no black in the Union Jack.

And the handclaps. The children's faces.
Handclaps.

C L E A R

The Rolex boys
This is your child benefit book.

Her

I've signed the back. I've signed it.
You get the money. You just go and pick it up.

They look at her
OK, but we fuck you as well.

She looks at them both
Go on then.

John out of the train. Vaults the wall onto the rooftops.
Down a drain pipe and onto the street running.

Kensington Palace.
The gardens. A picture of Diana.
Melody on the bench drumming.

Hopkins in the office. Everything neat.
His clean blotter. Spotless. Centred. A pen.
He writes C L E A R and leaves.

John down into the underground. Walking.
Approaching a barrier. A black man steps out.
Smiling

Where you going bro?
I have an appointment.
You have a ticket.

John is past him

I don't need one.

Hopkins in a car. At Melody's office.
With official driver. Through the barrier.

A girl helping the smackheads dress for the
government man. Nervous. Hands them Vaseline.
With a grimace.

As much of this city as you want.
Day time in the park.

John over the barriers with a leap.
Through the traffic. That pedestrian almost submerged by the buses and taxis
and bikes and vans.

Sean in the back of a cab. Oxford Street and Marble Arch.

Hopkins out of the offices and the car at Hyde Park Corner.

Melody in the sunlight. The helicopter above.

183

C L E A R

Sean at Marble Arch. Hopkins at Hyde Park Corner.

Melody by the Palace. John clear of the traffic and onto the grass.

They're walking. They're walking. Melody drums.

The girls go into the room with the government men.

The Palace and Melody. All around the people.

And Sean and Hopkins, and John is sweating.

Melody stands up.
John in the distance.

Hopkins ungainly and puffing.
Sean coming across.

Laughter and madness as the whip lashes out.
They're beating them.

185

CLEAR

A black woman on the bench
Shirlon. It's Shirlon.
John is passing her. Passing her.
She calls
John.
He turns to her.

Sean is there. There.
The metal to the temple.
Hopkins' lips.
The whip on the flesh.
A grunt delivered with each blow.
Two men grunting.

See the sky. The sky.

The sky.

After the gunshot.

From the sky, the body, crumpled.

The sky and Melody.

Then Hopkins' lips breaking into the smile.

The sky and the city.

Handclaps from the children.

Hand claps.

And they're beating the junkies.

Letting go on those girls.

And the Rolex boys are screaming.

Sirens are screaming. Its maximum pitch

Do the wall, do the wall.

The government men are beating them.

Blood on the walls. More blood on the walls.

The car is driven at speed.

187

The Rolex boy is shouting
Do it. Do it.
to the driver.
Sean on the bridge walking the parapet.
The sirens.
The Rolex boys scream past. And the police.
The car hits the wall.
Sean says
CLEAR
as he jumps.

The match is dropped.

The flag is burnt.

189

I wrote C L E A R more than twenty years ago.

Since then, on the surface, some things have changed.

Below that, nothing has changed.

It is also a love story. Maybe all stories are.

A very special thanks to Iain, Pat, Zion, Vikki for doing this.

Ray Leigh

Ray Leigh was born in London and grew up in south Essex.

By age 20 he was back, living in Camden Town, to the soundtrack of the Clash, the Sex Pistols, David Bowie and someone somewhere playing reggae.

The early 90s were times of turmoil, inner city riots, AIDS wiping out a generation of gay men, strikes, and wars. Trafalgar Square was ablaze as the poll tax protesters looted the West End and the murder of Stephen Lawrence was set to expose the racist underbelly of British society.

It was a testing time to be involved in youth work in north west London. As an outsider perhaps Ray was more sensitive to the way things were in the inner city communities. It seemed there were a lot of stories that were not getting told.

On the face of it the internet and mobile phones seemed to generate change but politicians' expenses, the financial crash and bankers' bail-out gave another view. 2012 might have been the London Olympics, but England had burned in riots only a year earlier.

But at 40 Ray had moved away from the pressures of working with young people and their families, studying English literature, making independent films and beginning to do what he'd always intended; to write.

Ray values authenticity, perhaps chasing truth as much as beauty. He sees elements in his work as a sort of reportage.

The borough where he lives is now marked by street corner shrines to the victims of gangland assassinations; and, 20 years after it was written, C L E A R is seeing the light of day.

BAD PRESS INK

Just when you thought it was safe
to go back in the bookstore...

www.badpress.ink

BAD PRESS iNK, publishers of niche, alternative and cult fiction

Visit

www.BADPRESS.iNK

for details of all our books, and sign up to
be notified of future releases and offers

YOUR INDEPENDENT BOOKSHOP NEEDS YOU!

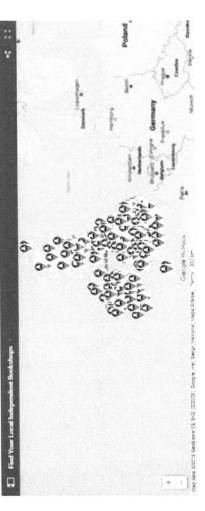

Find Your Local Independent Bookshops

Help us support local independent bookshops, visit:

www.BADPRESS.iNK/bookshops

to find your local bookshop.